For David and Amelia
M.W.

For Charlie
B.F.

This edition published 1999 by Walker Books Ltd
87 Vauxhall Walk, London SE11 5HJ

Text © 1991 Martin Waddell
Illustrations © 1991, 1999 Barbara Firth

First hardback edition 1991; reprinted 1991, 1996
First paperback edition 1994; reprinted 1995 (three times), 1998, 1999 (twice)

This paperback edition published 2000

This book has been typeset in Monotype Columbus.

Printed in Hong Kong

British Library Cataloguing in Publication Data
A catalogue record for this book is
available from the British Library.

ISBN 0-7445-7297-5

LET'S GO HOME, LITTLE BEAR

Martin Waddell

Illustrated by

Barbara Firth

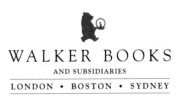

WALKER BOOKS
AND SUBSIDIARIES
LONDON · BOSTON · SYDNEY

Once there were two bears,
Big Bear and Little Bear.

Big Bear is the big bear

and Little Bear is the little bear.

They went for a walk in the woods.

They walked and they walked and

they walked until Big Bear said,

"Let's go home, Little Bear."

So they started back home on the

path through the woods.

PLOD PLOD PLOD

went Big Bear, plodding along.

Little Bear ran on in front,

jumping and sliding

and having great fun.

And then…

Little Bear stopped

and he listened

and then he turned round

and he looked.

"Come on, Little Bear," said Big Bear,

but Little Bear didn't stir.

"I thought I heard something!" Little Bear said.

"What did you hear?" said Big Bear.

"Plod, plod, plod," said Little Bear.

"I think it's a Plodder!"

Big Bear turned round and

he listened and looked.

No Plodder was there.

"Let's go home, Little Bear," said Big Bear.

"The plod was my feet in the snow."

They set off again on the path

through the woods.

PLOD PLOD PLOD

went Big Bear with Little Bear

walking beside him,

just glancing a bit, now and again.

And then…

Little Bear stopped

and he listened

and then he turned round

and he looked.

"Come on, Little Bear," said Big Bear,

but Little Bear didn't stir.

"I thought I heard something!"

Little Bear said.

"What did you hear?" said Big Bear.

"Drip, drip, drip," said Little Bear.

"I think it's a Dripper!"

Big Bear turned round, and
he listened and looked.
No Dripper was there.
"Let's go home, Little Bear,"
said Big Bear.
"That was the ice as it
dripped in the stream."

They set off again on the

path through the woods.

PLOD PLOD PLOD

went Big Bear with Little Bear

closer beside him.

And then…

Little Bear stopped

and he listened

and then he turned round

and he looked.

"Come on, Little Bear," said Big Bear,
  but Little Bear didn't stir.
"I know I heard something this time!"
  Little Bear said.
"What did you hear?" said Big Bear.
"Plop, plop, plop," said Little Bear.
"I think it's a Plopper."

Big Bear turned round,

and he listened and looked.

No Plopper was there.

"Let's go home, Little Bear,"

said Big Bear.

"That was the snow plopping

down from a branch."

PLOD PLOD PLOD

went Big Bear along the path

through the woods.

But Little Bear walked

slower and slower

and at last he sat

down in the snow.

"Come on, Little Bear," said Big Bear.

"It is time we were both back home."

But Little Bear sat and said nothing.

"Come on and be carried,"

said Big Bear.

Big Bear put Little Bear
high up on his back,
and set off down the path
through the woods.

WOO WOO WOO

"It is only the wind, Little Bear,"
said Big Bear and he walked
on down the path.

CREAK CREAK CREAK

"It is only the trees, Little Bear,"
said Big Bear and he walked
on down the path.

PLOD PLOD PLOD

"It is only the sound of my feet
again," said Big Bear, and he
plodded on and on and on
until they came back home
to their cave.

Big Bear and Little Bear
went down into the dark,
the dark of their own
Bear Cave.

"Just stay there, Little Bear,"
said Big Bear, putting
Little Bear in the Bear Chair
with a blanket to keep him warm.
Big Bear stirred up the fire from
the embers and lighted the lamps
and made the Bear Cave
all cosy again.
"Now tell me a story,"
Little Bear said.

And Big Bear sat down in the Bear Chair

with Little Bear curled on his lap.

And he told a story of Plodders

and Drippers and Ploppers

and the sounds of the snow

in the woods,

and this Little Bear

and this Big Bear

plodding all the way …

HOME